The Silver Sword

Dan Lee spends his time travelling between Asia and Britain. A wing chun master, he also trains in kickboxing and ju-jitsu.

Books in The Tangshan Tigers series

THE STOLEN JADE
THE GOLDEN KEY
THE INVISIBLE CLOUD
THE SILENT ENEMY
THE LIGHTNING STING
THE SILVER SHADOW

TANGSHAN TIGERS

The Silver Shadow

Dan Lee

PUFFIN

With special thanks to Brandon Robshaw

To Karen

PUFFIN BOOKS

Published by the Penguin Group
Penguin Books Ltd, 80 Strand, London WC2R 0RL, England
Penguin Group (USA) Inc., 375 Hudson Street, New York, New York 10014, USA
Penguin Group (Canada), 90 Eglinton Avenue East, Suite 700, Toronto, Ontario, Canada M4P 2Y3
(a division of Pearson Penguin Canada Inc.)
Penguin Ireland, 25 St Stephen's Green, Dublin 2, Ireland (a division of Penguin Books Ltd)
Penguin Group (Australia), 250 Camberwell Road, Camberwell, Victoria 3124, Australia
(a division of Pearson Australia Group Pty Ltd)
Penguin Books India Pvt Ltd, 11 Community Centre, Panchsheel Park, New Delhi – 110 017, India
Penguin Group (NZ), 67 Apollo Drive, Rosedale, North Shore 0632, New Zealand
(a division of Pearson New Zealand Ltd)
Penguin Books (South Africa) (Pty) Ltd, 24 Sturdee Avenue, Rosebank,
Johannesburg 2196, South Africa

Penguin Books Ltd, Registered Offices: 80 Strand, London WC2R 0RL, England

puffinbooks.com

First published 2008
1

Series created by Working Partners Ltd, London
Text copyright © Working Partners Ltd, 2008
All rights reserved

The moral right of the author has been asserted

Set in Bembo
Typeset by Palimpsest Book Production Limited, Grangemouth, Stirlingshire
Made and printed in England by Clays Ltd, St Ives plc

British Library Cataloguing in Publication Data
A CIP catalogue record for this book is available from the British Library

ISBN: 978-0-141-32489-0

www.greenpenguin.co.uk

Penguin Books is committed to a sustainable future
for our business, our readers and our planet.
The book in your hands is made from paper
certified by the Forest Stewardship Council.

CONTENTS

A MYSTERY SURFACES

'Newton's three laws. Does anyone know what they are?' asked Mrs Tyler. Shawn immediately put his hand up. He was heavily into science.

'Oh good, someone knows,' said Mrs Tyler. 'The first law is that a body at rest will stay at rest until something moves it – or if it's moving it will carry on moving until something stops it. Is that what you were going to say, Shawn?'

'Er, yeah, and the second law is –'

'Oh yes, the second law – a moving object will accelerate if acted on by a force,' said Mrs Tyler, cutting across Shawn. Matt had to smile at the frown of frustration that crossed Shawn's face. Mrs Tyler asked a lot of questions, but always answered them herself; she'd rather listen to her own voice than anyone else's.

'And the third law, of course,' Mrs Tyler went on, 'is that every action has an equal and opposite reaction . . .'

Right, thought Matt, *Mrs Tyler's action is to drone on and on, and my reaction is to fall asleep . . .*

Matt had just returned from London where he'd captained the Beijing International Academy martial arts squad against the Kensington International Academy. They'd won a narrow victory – and Matt and the Tangshan Tigers had also found time to catch an international diamond thief while they were there. The Tangshan Tigers were a secret crime-fighting gang that Matt had formed with his friends Shawn Hung, Catarina Ribeiro and Olivier Girard. It had been a great adventure, but after all the excitement Matt was glad to get back to normality. It was just a pity that normality included Mrs Tyler's physics lessons.

Matt allowed his thoughts to drift back to his fight against Adam Bates in the tournament. Adam was his old enemy, a bully who'd given him a hard time at school when he was younger. No matter how many times he relived the experience of beating Adam, it was still uplifting.

The match had been poised at 5-5 and Matt needed to win to take the tournament for BIA. He remembered that first point he'd scored, when he'd caught Adam with a front kick and seen a grudging respect dawn in his opponent's eyes.

Then there was the part where Adam had got him down and nearly pinned him, but Matt, using the *Chi Sao* principle Chang had taught him, had anticipated Adam's movement and freed himself just in time.

His defensive work against Adam's persistent attacks, the blocks, the counter-strikes . . . Then that tense moment after the bout where they'd stood panting side by side, waiting for the judge's verdict . . . And the sweet relief that flooded through Matt when the judges announced him as the winner!

That was a memory that would never get boring, no matter how often he re-ran it.

Matt was jolted out of his daydream as the door to the classroom burst open. Mr Wu, the Principal, stood there. Normally a neat and dapper man, he looked as though he'd got dressed in a hurry today – his tie was knotted loosely and his hair was dishevelled.

He snapped his fingers. 'Mrs Tyler – you have members of martial arts squad in this class?' he rapped out in a loud voice.

Mrs Tyler blinked. 'Er, why yes, but –'

'Where are they?' he demanded.

Matt, the other Tangshan Tigers and Carl Warrick slowly raised their hands. Matt exchanged a puzzled glance with Olivier, who was sitting nearest him. It wasn't like Mr Wu to interrupt lessons in this way. By this stage in the academic year, Mr Wu should know who was in the martial arts squad – he'd always been extremely proud of their achievements.

'Good. You must all leave this class and come with me!'

'Excuse me,' said Mrs Tyler. 'I wasn't told

about this, and the class have important exams in only two days, as you know.'

Mr Wu took a step towards her, so quickly that he knocked into a bowl of water on a nearby table. It fell to the floor and smashed, spattering Mr Wu's suit trousers with water. The bowl had contained a propeller-driven model boat – an experiment Mrs Tyler had set up to illustrate Newton's third law. Mrs Tyler bent to pick up the pieces.

'Leave that!' snapped Mr Wu. 'Tidy up later. Let me ask you a question, Mrs Tyler – who is the Principal? Is it you? Or is it me?'

Matt felt shocked. He had never heard Mr Wu speak to a member of staff like this before.

'It's you, Mr Wu, of course,' Mrs Tyler said, her face flushing.

'Oh, I thought perhaps the board of governors had appointed you in my place without informing me,' said Mr Wu with heavy sarcasm. 'Since we agree that I am the Principal, perhaps you could kindly allow me to do my job? These squad members are coming with me for some extra training. If you have a problem with that, you may put it in writing. And don't forget to write "PS I resign" at the end of the letter.'

Mrs Tyler did not reply. Matt thought he saw her lower lip trembling.

'Her lessons might be boring,' he whispered to Olivier, 'but she doesn't deserve to be spoken to like that!'

Olivier nodded.

'Come on!' said Mr Wu impatiently to the squad members, snapping his fingers again. 'Follow me!'

Matt rose from his seat. He exchanged glances with the other Tigers. Olivier raised his eyebrows; Shawn shrugged. Catarina murmured, 'Go figure' to Matt in a low voice. It would have been good to miss double physics under other circumstances, but not like this. The only person who didn't seem bothered was Carl; Matt could see him grinning at having escaped from the lesson.

Mr Wu set off down the corridor at a brisk pace, his shoes clicking on the polished floor. Matt, Olivier, Catarina and Carl followed. Shawn lingered behind in the classroom a moment. He caught up with the others at the end of the corridor.

'What kept you?' asked Olivier.

Shawn grinned. 'Just fixing something up.'

'No talking – hurry, hurry, hurry!' said Mr Wu.

They had to hurry to keep up with him, jogging past framed photos of the school's winning sports teams from down the years.

'What's with him?' said Catarina in an urgent whisper.

'He's always been a bit competitive about the martial arts team,' said Olivier. 'But not like this.'

'Got out the wrong side of the bed?' whispered Matt.

'But why the extra training?' said Shawn. 'We're not due to fight another tournament for ages –'

'What? What are you guys saying?' asked Carl loudly.

'Silence!' shouted Mr Wu over his shoulder. 'Other students are in class, kindly do not disturb them!'

They proceeded in silence until they got to the *kwoon,* or training hall. It had a high ceiling, and there was a scarlet dragon painted across the length of one wall. But the most impressive feature was the big white combat mat in the middle of the hall. The rest of the squad were already waiting there: Lola, Wolfgang, Jahmal, Paolo, Abdul and Andrei. They all looked as confused as Matt felt. There was no sign of their coach, Chang Sifu.

'Here we all are,' said Mr Wu. He rubbed his hands together in a satisfied manner; he seemed a lot calmer now. 'It is very important for the martial arts team to train hard to remain in tiptop condition. And I am sure you would rather spend your time in the *kwoon* than doing boring lessons, wouldn't you? I know that is what I would have preferred when I was a schoolboy.'

It was an unusual attitude for the Principal of an Academy to take, thought Matt. He knew that Mr Wu loved collecting trophies to display in his office, but he had never gone as far as interrupting lessons before – especially when, as Shawn had pointed out, there wasn't even a tournament in the offing. And Wu was every bit as proud of top exam results as he was of martial arts successes.

'On to the mat,' said Mr Wu, gesturing. 'Start training routines. You have until lunchtime.'

'But Chang Sifu's not here,' said Shawn. 'There's no one to coach us.'

'Chang will be here later. Until then I suggest you waste no time, but begin training at once. You must know the training drills by now — you are not infants. Are you incapable of working independently?'

'But Chang's taught us lots of different training exercises,' said Catarina. 'We don't know which —'

'Let me ask you all a question!' said Mr Wu impatiently. 'Would you like to spend the morning cleaning out all the toilets in the building? Would you enjoy that?'

'No, sir,' said Lola.

'Then do as you are told! That goes for all of you – understood?'

'Yes, sir,' they all chanted. Matt muttered agreement along with the rest of the squad; there didn't seem anything else to do.

'Then start training!' their principal snapped. Mr Wu turned on his heel and walked out briskly.

Everyone stood staring at each other, nonplussed.

'Well,' said Matt, deciding that somebody ought to take the lead, 'I guess the first thing to do is get changed. Then we'll work out some training routines.'

Their martial arts suits were kept in their lockers in the changing rooms. Within five minutes, the squad was changed and back in the *kwoon*.

'Right,' said Matt, 'we'd better start with

a warm-up. How about a few leg-stretches –'

'Wait a second!' protested Carl. 'Who put you in charge? Huh?'

'No one, but –'

'Matt was captain in the last tournament,' said Lola.

'Yeah, but he's not captain now!' said Carl. He pointed at himself. 'I reckon I should be in charge.'

'Why?' asked Paolo.

'I'm the fittest,' said Carl, 'and I know more about training than you guys, 'cause I learned from my dad.'

'Yeah, not that I'm a know-it-all or anything!' said Olivier in his perfect imitation of Carl's voice. 'But being the great Carl Warrick I do happen to know everything there is to know –'

'Hey, quit making fun of my accent!' said Carl, raising his voice above the laughter.

'I'm not making fun of your accent,' Olivier explained. 'I'm making fun of *you*.'

Carl's face reddened. He clenched his fists. 'I've had about enough of your funny cracks. Wanna make something of it?'

Carl took two strides towards Olivier and eyeballed him at close range. Matt saw a muscle twitching in his jaw. Olivier didn't flinch, but returned Carl's aggressive stare.

The rest of the squad pressed around them, getting excited at the prospect of a fight.

'OK, OK,' said Matt, pushing to the front. He could see things turning nasty. 'This isn't worth fighting over – back off, you guys.' He pulled Olivier away by the arm.

'Yeah, get your mate to pull you out of trouble, that's right,' said Carl sarcastically.

'I think Olivier should apologize,' said Andrei, unexpectedly pitching in on Carl's side.

'What are you, crazy?' said Olivier. 'Why should I apologize to him?' Olivier threw a dismissive wave in Carl's direction.

'It's Carl who should apologize,' said Catarina. 'For being such an idiot!'

'They should both apologize to each other,' said Lola, folding her arms.

'I think they should just fight and sort it out once and for all!' said Wolfgang.

The noise of raised voices filled the *kwoon*.

'Everybody, calm down!' shouted Matt, struggling to make himself heard above the din.

The door opened. Chang Sifu stepped into the hall.

At once, the noise level dropped. The students looked down in shame as Chang walked into their midst. As usual, their tutor brought an atmosphere of calm into the room with him. He was slim, of athletic build, with greying hair, and walked with an easy grace. His face was expressionless.

'Please to form training lines,' he said quietly.

Without a word, the squad formed into their training lines.

Chang Sifu did not speak. He stood there regarding them. *This is torture*, Matt thought, watching his tutor's face for a clue as to what he might be thinking. *Say something! Tell us off! Anything.*

'I am disappointed,' Chang Sifu said finally. 'You have trained together for some months now. You have fought side by side in difficult contests. I thought sense of unity would have grown. I do not expect to find you arguing in this petty manner – coming almost to blows!'

'We're really sorry, Sifu,' Matt said respectfully. 'Things got out of hand. It won't happen again. But we're all feeling a bit confused today. We shouldn't even really be here; we're supposed to be in class preparing for our exams.'

Chang Sifu inclined his head. 'I know. But such is the situation; you must make best of it. Perhaps man who brought you here today has done you a favour.'

Man? thought Matt. *Why doesn't Chang Sifu name names? We all know this is down to Mr Wu.*

'How d'you make that out?' asked Carl sulkily.

'He put you in unexpected situation. Martial artist must be adaptable. In fight, you must be aware of many things at once – stance, balance, defence, weak spots to protect, distance from opponent, opponent's style of fighting and so on – yet still ready to expect unexpected. Is life so different? Here too you must deal with many things at same time. If you can focus on training today, with exams looming, you prove you have learned that lesson.'

Matt nodded. As always, he found Chang's words inspired him. He saw Catarina, who was standing beside him, nodding too, and heard murmurs of agreement all round. The only person who did not seem impressed was Carl, who rolled his eyeballs and heaved a loud sigh.

Chang gave no sign of noticing. 'Let us put your focus to test then. Question: what lessons do you miss this morning?'

'Science,' said Matt. 'We were doing physics with Mrs Tyler.'

'We were doing geography,' said Jahmal.

'I see,' said Chang. 'Science and geography.' He looked thoughtful for a moment. 'This morning let us have free session. That is, each person to repeat sequence of moves from your own chosen discipline. Karate students, such as Carl, Andrei, Abdul, perform a *kata* – kung fu students, like Olivier, Jahmal, a form. Students of take-down styles – judo, ju-jitsu – will work in pairs to practise throws and holds. Start with short simple sequence and extend, gradually stretch yourself, move out of comfort zone.'

Soon the *kwoon* was filled with the sound of feet moving on the mat, and grunts and hard breathing as students threw themselves into their routines. Matt began a pattern, a sequence of familiar tae kwon-do moves he'd often used when training alone: a jab, a single-handed block, a crescent kick, a double-handed block, a step back and turn, then a reverse kick.

He noticed Chang moving among the students, deftly avoiding the windmilling arms and legs, stopping and quietly asking questions. Matt began to feel curious. What was Chang asking them? Several students seemed puzzled by the questions; he saw Paolo frown and lose the rhythm of his movements. Chang encouraged him to carry on with the sequence and waited for Paolo to answer. Then he nodded and moved on.

He stopped close by Matt, just as Matt was about to turn for his reverse kick.

'The angle of incidence equals – what?' he murmured.

Matt was so surprised he almost lost his balance. 'Er – the angle of deflection!'

'That is correct.'

He moved on and Matt heard him say to Lola. 'What is an oxbow lake?'

Matt was so amazed that he almost burst out laughing. Chang was testing them in their exam subjects, at the same time as putting them through their training. As well as being an expert in several martial arts, he also knew the science and geography syllabuses!

'Does Chang know everything?' he whispered to Shawn.

'It looks like it.' said Shawn.

'Whew,' said Matt. 'I'm exhausted!'

'Me also,' said Catarina, leaning back in her chair and stretching out her long legs. It was evening and the Tangshan Tigers had gathered in Matt's room. On the computer monitor a screen-saver showed two tae kwon-do fighters in combat.

Matt had invited the Tigers after supper to discuss the day's events. Matt shared a room with Johnny Goldberg, but Johnny had just come down with a bad dose of flu and was staying in the sanatorium until he was better.

'What a day!' said Shawn. 'First that extra session this morning –'

'Training and trying to answer science questions at the same time!' said Olivier.

'Then lessons after lunch,' said Catarina.

'And then – can you believe it, another training session, by order of Mr Wu, before supper!' said Matt.

'At least it'll get us fit,' said Olivier, sitting on the edge of Matt's bed.

'Yeah, but will it get us through the exams?' said Shawn.

'We could be in trouble,' said Matt sombrely. 'I know Chang was helping us revise this morning, but it's not the same as being in the lesson!'

Shawn grinned. 'Good job you got me then, isn't it?' He burrowed in the backpack that lay on the floor at his feet and pulled out a small black device. It had a lens set into its face.

'What's that?'

'Digital video recorder. I set it up just before we got dragged out of Mrs Tyler's class this morning.'

'You mean – it's got the whole lesson on it?' said Matt.

'Sure. Let's connect it to your computer and we can watch and learn!'

The bedrooms at the Beijing Academy were each equipped with a computer with a high-definition, widescreen monitor mounted on the wall. Shawn plugged his digital recorder into the port of the desktop. A beautifully clear, crisp image of Mrs Tyler standing at the front of the class appeared on the monitor.

Catarina giggled. 'I never thought I'd be glad to sit through one of Mrs Tyler's lessons.'

'It gets better,' said Shawn. 'Look!'

He pressed a button on the handset and

subtitles appeared across the bottom of the screen. 'If moving objects keep on moving, as the first law says, why do things stop? Because of the forces of gravity and air resistance. In outer space, there is nothing to stop an object, say a comet, going on forever . . .'

'Wait!' said Olivier. 'I want to write that down.'

'Sure,' said Shawn, pausing the recording. Mrs Tyler froze in mid-sentence with her mouth open. Olivier and Catarina noted down her words. Matt concentrated on committing them to his photographic memory. 'But here's the best thing,' went on Shawn. 'When we get to the boring bits –'

'There'll be quite a few of those with Mrs Tyler,' said Matt. The others laughed.

'Sure, but look, we can fast-forward it!'

'Neat,' said Catarina. 'This is the way I like to study!'

With Shawn pausing the most important parts and skipping over the boring bits in between, they covered the whole lesson and noted all the key points in twenty minutes.

'We'll be OK if the three laws of motion come up in the exam, anyway,' said Matt, feeling cheered.

'Yeah – but let's hope we don't miss no more classes,' said Catarina.

'I wouldn't be surprised if we do,' said Olivier. 'Looks like Mr Wu's got a bee in his bonnet about training us up.'

'But why?' said Catarina. 'He's acting very weird – I don't get it!'

'When's our next match?' asked Shawn.

'Over a month away,' said Matt promptly. He had memorized the fixture list. 'Home match against the Singapore Intercontinental School.'

Olivier whistled. 'They're hot stuff. Unbeaten this season.'

'So are we,' Matt pointed out.

'Sure, but it's a tough fixture.'

'I still don't see why Mr Wu's acting so strange,' said Shawn. 'The match against Kensington was tough too, but he wasn't pulling us out of lessons a month before it.'

'Maybe,' said Catarina thoughtfully, 'he's got some kinda grudge against the Singapore School? You remember how much he wanted to beat Shanghai? Maybe it's like that – there's something personal going on here.'

'Could be,' said Olivier. 'But if so, why? It's a mystery.'

'And mysteries –' began Shawn.

'Are a job for the Tangshan Tigers!' finished Matt.

A NEW COACH

'I'm terribly sorry, I'm afraid I can't let you in,' said Mrs Barraclough, standing in her classroom doorway.

'Excuse me?' said Matt. After yesterday's strange events he had been hoping things would get back to normal.

'I'm sorry,' said Mrs Barraclough again. 'It's no admittance for you today – that's what I've been told. I've already sent Carl Warrick away.'

Matt and the Tigers hovered in the

corridor outside Mrs Barraclough's room, unsure what to do with themselves. Mrs Barraclough smiled apologetically, running her hand through her frizzy hair.

'But you said we'd do quadratic equations today,' said Shawn. 'I was really looking forward to it!'

'It's such a pity,' said Mrs Barraclough. 'I'm afraid you'll have to do the quadratic equations another day. I've been asked to tell you to go to martial arts training on the school field – I'd let you come in if I could, but Mr Wu said . . .'

Her voice trailed away.

'It's all right,' Matt said to her. 'Can't be helped.' He turned to the others. 'Come on, guys. We'd better change and get out there.'

The rest of the squad were all out on the field when they arrived, jogging round the track.

'Yo, Matt!' said Lola as she ran past. 'What lesson you missing?'

'No talking at this time!' rapped out a woman in a blue tracksuit. She bounced up and down at the side of the track, jogging on the spot. She had short blonde hair, an athletic physique, an American accent, and was carrying a clipboard. There was no sign of Mr Wu or of Chang.

'Get moving!' she called out. 'Pick it up! Come on, you're not trying. Lengthen the stride – I don't wanna see you shambling round like zombies! You lot –' she pointed at the Tangshan Tigers – 'fall in and get with it!'

'Excuse me,' said Matt, 'what's going on?' Then, in case that had sounded too abrupt, he added politely, 'I'm Matt James, by the way.'

'Hi there, Matt James. You're probably wondering who I am. Well, I'll tell you.' She

29

broke off to call to Wolfgang as he came jogging past. 'Pick your feet up! That's it!' She turned back to the Tigers. 'I'm Megan Walker – your new fitness and motivation coach.'

She was still energetically jogging up and down on the spot without the slightest sign of getting out of breath.

'But – Master Chang is our coach!' said Catarina.

A cold hand of dread gripped Matt's heart – it had happened once before that Chang had suddenly been replaced with no explanation. Could Mr Wu have done it again?

'He's still your coach for all the technical stuff,' said Megan Walker. Matt felt a gush of relief. 'But I'm here to get you fighting fit and ready to rumble!'

'Hold on one little mineeto –' began Catarina.

'Spare me the backchat. Just get on that track and start running.'

Catarina's eyes flashed and Matt could see she was about to burst out in protest. He quickly laid a hand on her arm and said in a low voice, 'Leave it for now.' Catarina pouted, but didn't say anything more.

'Of course we'll start running,' he said politely to the new coach. 'Come on, guys, let's go!'

He led them round the track at a brisk pace. Catarina loped alongside him and when they had passed the first bend, she said, 'Why didn't you let me tell that woman we don't need a motivational coach? We got Chang – he doesn't just do "technical stuff"!'

'Right!' said Shawn. 'No one could motivate us better than Chang – doesn't she know anything about the set-up here?'

'I totally agree, but it's not that simple,' said

Matt, beginning to breathe harder as they rounded the second bend. In the background they could still hear Megan Walker shouting at the runners. 'She's here now. Complaining won't get us anywhere. Mr Wu's not going to sack her because we don't like it.'

'Matt's right,' said Olivier. 'We have to work with her, so we'd better make the best of it.'

'But she's taking over Chang's job – or part of it!' said Shawn. 'How do you think he feels?'

'Chang's always told us we've got to be disciplined, keep focus,' said Matt. 'And to control our emotions. He wants us to be able to deal with the unexpected – and that's what we've gotta do.'

They had completed the first lap now and were just drawing level with Megan Walker again. 'Faster!' she shouted as they ran past. 'Show me what you got!'

'Mind you,' panted Matt, once they were out of earshot again, 'it's not gonna be easy!'

Matt had lost count of how many laps they had run when he saw Chang Sifu himself, with Mr Wu, standing next to Megan Walker at the side of the track. He nudged Shawn. 'Look, he's here.'

'Thank goodness for that,' said Shawn.

'Let's stop and say hello,' said Catarina.

They slowed down and came to a halt in front of Chang.

'Good morning, Sifu,' said Matt, as he and the others performed the traditional Chinese sign of respect, touching the right fist against the left palm at chest height. Master Chang returned the gesture.

'Hey! Did I say you could stop?' snapped Megan Walker.

'No, she did NOT say you could stop!' said Mr Wu. 'You must do what your motivational coach tells you – if she says run, you RUN!'

'Indeed,' said Chang quietly. 'It is important to carry out task given. But students have run many laps now. It is not good to overexert students. Perhaps it is time for break?' Matt saw him look at Megan Walker for agreement; she met his eye, but did not answer.

Mr Wu burst out in a ragged, angry voice, 'Chang, you had better keep your NOSE OUT of this business! You are here to teach the fancy moves, but Miss Walker is the motivational coach and she knows her job and you must not INTERFERE!'

Matt clenched his fists; he felt rage rising inside him. He wanted to shout at Mr Wu that the BIA martial arts team answered to their coach, not Wu or Walker or anyone else; their loyalty was to Chang Sifu. But before he could speak he saw Chang glance at him and imperceptibly shake his head. Chang appeared calm as always, completely unfazed by Mr Wu's outburst. Megan Walker looked slightly embarrassed; she had even stopped bouncing up and down on the spot.

The rest of the team came running up to join them. They must have heard Mr Wu's rant because they all looked worried.

'Have we finished?' asked Carl loudly.

'Has Miss Walker told you to finish?' barked Mr Wu. 'No? Has anyone? Are you hearing imaginary voices? Why stop then?'

Olivier nudged Matt. 'The guy's seriously stressed out,' he murmured. 'He didn't even dress properly this morning. Have you seen the state of his collar? It's filthy.'

Matt inched a little closer, pretending to be jogging on the spot, and saw that Mr Wu's collar, which would normally be gleaming white, was stained with a yellowish-tan powder. It wasn't dirt, he realized. It was . . . make-up? Matt had always known that the Principal was vain, but wearing face powder? What had come over Mr Wu? Before Matt could answer Olivier, however, Mr Wu had begun talking again, this time in a slightly calmer voice.

'Since you are all here, I will take this moment to make an important announcement, before you recommence your training. It is vitally important that you put in one hundred per cent effort, for your next tournament will take place sooner than originally planned. In fact, it will take place in three days' time.'

There was a shocked murmur from the team. Even Chang Sifu furrowed his brow slightly.

'Three days?' muttered Shawn. 'That's crazy!'

'I know!' said Matt. 'It gives us hardly any time −'

'QUIET, please! I have proposed the new date to the Principal of the Singapore Intercontinental School and he has agreed, so there is absolutely no point in arguing.'

Matt raised his hand. 'Why was the date changed, sir?'

'For good reasons that are no concern of yours.'

'But that doesn't give us enough time to prepare −' said Matt.

'It gives you ample time if you are not LAZY!' said Mr Wu angrily. Two bright red spots appeared on his cheeks. 'So get on with doing what Miss Walker tells you and do not waste my time in pointless disputation!'

He turned abruptly and walked away, striding briskly over the grass.

Megan Walker clapped her hands. 'Another five laps, and this time do it like you mean it – go!'

As Matt turned to resume running, he saw Chang was watching him. For a split second their eyes met. Chang's lips silently formed a word.

Patience.

Then Chang turned and walked away.

Chang was right, Matt knew. Yes, he would be patient. But there was something funny going on here. And he meant to find out what it was.

'OK, gather round,' said Megan Walker as the last stragglers – Wolfgang, Abdul, Paolo and Jahmal – finished the last lap. The squad slumped or sat on the grass.

'Oh, no no no no no!' said Megan. 'No flop-downs, please!' She was still bouncing about on the balls of her feet, as fresh as a daisy. 'Up up up up up.'

Slowly, the squad got to their feet. Wolfgang stood bent over, with his hands on his knees.

'Stand up straight!' said Megan, pointing at him. 'You guys are seriously lacking in cardiovascular fitness and I aim to put that right! OK?' No one said anything. 'I said, is that OK?' Megan repeated.

The squad nodded or mumbled agreement. Matt wished Megan would stop bouncing about. The woman seemed unable to keep still.

'Now listen up, guys!' said Miss Walker. She gave the squad a big grin. 'I got something for you.'

She rummaged about in her sports bag,

then straightened up holding a pile of DVDs. 'This is a motivational film. One for each of you. It's designed to inspire you – make you full of self-belief, bursting with self-confidence. You watch this whenever you're not training – watch it before breakfast, at lunchtime, in your breaks, before you go to bed at night – and, well, you'll see the results. That's a promise!'

She handed the DVDs round.

The team stared disbelievingly at the slim packages.

'Enjoy!' said Megan. 'Now, go and get changed.'

As they walked away, Matt glanced back and saw that Megan had started running round the track, her arms and legs going like pistons.

He nudged Catarina and pointed.

'Is she for real?' said Catarina.

They both laughed. But the seriousness of the situation soon settled on Matt.

'Only three days to prepare for the match!' he said to Catarina as they were walking into the changing rooms.

'It's the same for the Singapore School, I guess.'

'Maybe,' said Matt. 'But have they got exams in three days, like us?'

And that wasn't all. Matt knew that the man shouting at them had been nothing like the Mr Wu they had come to know. Something was seriously wrong with the Principal – but what?

TAKING A GAMBLE

Matt was tired. He sat at a table in the refectory with the Tangshan Tigers, twisting the spoon in his porridge.

'I've never felt less ready for an exam,' he said.

'I know what you mean,' said Shawn. 'I was going to do some revision last night, but I was so tired after the evening session in the *kwoon*, I couldn't keep my eyes open.'

'Well, we'll just have to do our best,' said Matt.

The electronic twangs of an amplified *guzheng*, the Chinese zither, sounded through the tannoys. Then Mr Wu's voice: 'School examinations will commence in fifteen minutes. Could all students please make their way to the Examination Hall.'

Matt pushed away his bowl of porridge and stood up. So did the others.

'Well – good luck, everyone!' said Matt.

'We're gonna need it,' said Catarina.

An hour later, Matt was sitting in the Examination Hall, staring at the screen in front of him. The only sounds were the shuffle of feet, the distant hum of the air-conditioner and the occasional cough. Mrs Barraclough and their history teacher, Mr Figgis, were invigilating.

The Examination Hall was a hi-tech building with soundproofed walls and tinted

windows to keep out the sun's glare. All the
desks had monitor screens set into them,
where the exam questions appeared, instead
of on question papers. A touchpad underneath
allowed you to key in your answers.

But Matt hadn't keyed anything in yet.
His mind was full of Mr Wu's strange
behaviour. Mr Wu had always taken delight
in the reflected glory from his martial arts
team. But until now he had never been so
bossy, so bad-tempered and so downright
unreasonable. It was as if some strange force
had taken him over. *Maybe he isn't well*,
thought Matt. *He's not himself. Maybe he
needs to see a doctor* . . .

He shook his head. He had to concentrate
on these quadratic equations. He forced
himself to focus on the questions. The
mysterious little x's and y's glimmered on the
screen, taunting him. It was all very well

having a photographic memory when there was anything for it to remember. But he had missed most of the work on quadratic equations and had only the vaguest idea how to solve them.

He looked up at the large digital clock set into the wall at the front. Seventeen minutes to go and he'd barely started.

He looked across at Olivier, who was sitting with his head in his hands. Olivier looked up, saw Matt, gestured at the screen in front of him and made a helpless face.

Matt nodded in sympathy. He looked back at his monitor. If he passed this exam it would be a miracle.

That evening, the Tangshan Tigers gathered in Matt's room.

'Well – how did everybody do?' asked Matt, with a rueful smile.

'I did terrible,' said Catarina frankly.

Olivier shook his head sadly. 'Disaster.'

'I'm worried,' said Shawn. 'Like, really worried. My score's gonna be so low, it'll go before the Academic Board, and then –'

'But they'll let us do retakes, won't they?' asked Matt anxiously. A feeling of dread ran through him at the thought of what his mum would say if he was expelled. 'The board wouldn't kick us out without giving us a second chance?'

'Probably not,' said Shawn. 'But if Wu's gonna make us do all this extra training, missing lessons all the time, we won't do any better in the retakes.'

'He might ease off after the match with Singapore,' suggested Olivier.

'Yeah, and he might not!' said Catarina. 'The guy's out of control. How do we know he won't fix up another tournament at three days' notice and make us work our butts off again?'

At that moment, the liquid notes of the *guzheng* sounded over the tannoy – cue for an announcement.

'This is a message for the martial arts team,' came Mr Wu's voice. 'The squad will report to the *kwoon* at six a.m. tomorrow morning, changed and ready for training. Repeat, six a.m. Lateness will not be tolerated. Thank you.'

There was a moment's pause, then the Tangshan Tigers burst out laughing. But it was painful, near-hysterical laughter.

'This is just – too much!' gasped Matt.

'Good job we can laugh,' said Olivier.

'Yeah, 'cause we'd cry if we didn't,' said Catarina.

'Seriously, though,' said Matt. 'We can't carry on like this.'

'How about we go on strike?' said Catarina suddenly. 'What would Mr Wu do then?'

'Put some reserves in,' said Olivier. 'And the BIA would get smashed.'

'But we have to do *something*!' said Matt.

'Yeah,' said Shawn. 'Wu's not only risking the team's success by all this over-training – he's putting our education at risk.'

'Here's what I think,' said Matt. 'We'll carry on training and we'll do everything we can to win the tournament. But in the meantime, why don't we investigate Mr Wu? There's something strange going on with him. Like, did anyone else spot he was wearing make-up yesterday?'

'No way!' said Shawn.

'Way,' said Matt.

'You're right, Matt,' said Catarina. 'Enough already. It's time for the Tangshan Tigers to investigate!'

She sprang to her feet.

'You mean – now?' said Olivier.

'Why not now?' said Matt. 'It's late – Mr Wu will have gone home for the night. Let's go to his office and have a look round!'

The lights in the corridors were slowly dimming. In a few minutes they would have reached the eerie blue glow that was the night-time setting – when all students were supposed to be in bed. Matt felt nervous as they made their way to Mr Wu's office. They had to hurry – if a teacher saw them prowling about this close to lights-out, they would be sent back to their dorms.

Fortunately, they reached the office without meeting anybody. The expensively varnished office door was in a plush reception area with leather sofas and potted plants.

Matt reached out for the handle – and jumped as the door suddenly swung open.

49

Mr Wu stood there, staring at the Tangshan Tigers with surprise and disapproval.

'What are you doing here?' he snapped. He glanced into the office over his shoulder — *as if there was something there he didn't want us to see*, thought Matt. 'It is late, you should be up in your rooms! You are in the martial arts squad, you have to get up early tomorrow!'

Olivier, as always, came to the rescue with a plausible story. 'We were on our way to do some late-night exercise. We thought we'd go outside and do some fitness training on the athletics track.'

Mr Wu looked suspicious. His eyes darted about behind his glasses, flicking from one Tangshan Tiger to the next. 'But this is not the way to the athletics track! Why do I find you outside my office?'

He's not going to buy it, thought Matt. *He's seen through us . . .!*

'We wouldn't go out to train at this time of night without asking your permission, sir,' said Olivier, with his most winning smile. 'We just came to see if it would be all right.'

'Ah,' said Mr Wu. The suspicious frown faded from his face. He pushed his glasses back up, which had slid down the bridge of his nose. 'It is good that you are so keen, er – I am sorry, what is your name?'

'Olivier Girard,' said Olivier, looking puzzled. Matt was taken aback too. How could Mr Wu not remember Olivier's name after all this time?

'Well, Olivier, and you others,' said Mr Wu, smiling genially now, 'I am glad to see such an attitude. I can't wait to see you hammering that Singapore team in two days' time! But I am sorry, you cannot go outside to train now – it is nearly lights-out.'

Mr Wu closed the office door behind him

and took a bunch of keys from his jacket pocket.

As Wu fumbled with his keys, Matt noticed something odd about their principal. He usually wore expensive, well-cut suits with razor-sharp creases. The suit he had on now was rumpled and not a perfect fit – the sleeves came down over his wrists. There were grease spots on the lapels. His steel spectacles looked a little wonky too, and as Matt watched he pushed them back up the bridge of his nose again. Mr Wu had always looked immaculate – but not any more. *There's something weird going on here*, thought Matt. *Why's he letting himself go like this?*

Mr Wu locked the office door, put the keys back in his pocket and pushed his jacket sleeves back from his wrists. 'Well, goodnight,' he said. He smiled, revealing a row of sharp teeth. 'Time for bed – don't be late for training tomorrow! Six a.m.!'

'Goodnight, sir,' said Olivier.

The Tangshan Tigers turned and walked away as if they were going to the dorms.

But they did not walk far. In the next corridor Matt beckoned his friends into the shadow of a stairwell.

'Let's wait here,' he whispered.

A minute later they were rewarded by the sight of Mr Wu walking briskly past. He looked preoccupied, staring at the floor. He turned the corner at the end of the corridor. They heard his footsteps die away.

'Anyone else notice his suit?' said Matt.

'Yes,' said Olivier. 'I've never seen him look so shabby.'

'There's definitely something weird going on,' said Shawn.

'Well,' said Matt, 'let's see what clues we can pick up in his study.'

They hurried back to the office.

'How are we going to get in?' asked Olivier. He rattled the door handle. 'He locked it, remember?'

'What about that universal key of yours, Shawn?' Matt asked. Shawn had a gadget that could open any lock.

Shawn shook his head. 'No can do. It needs a nitrogen refill.'

'There must be *something* we can do to get in,' said Matt, frustrated. The clue to Wu's strange behaviour might be just on the other side of the door. But how were they to get at it?

'Leave it with me!' said Catarina.

'What are you –' began Matt. But Catarina was already silently loping away down the dimly lit passage.

The remaining Tangshan Tigers looked at each other, mystified.

Five minutes went by. Suddenly there were noises from the other side of the office door. Was that a window opening? Matt and the others glanced at each other. They heard the tread of light footsteps. Then a click, and Matt saw the door handle turn.

The door opened. Catarina stood there, grinning broadly.

'How on earth did you get in?' demanded Matt.

'Through the window, how else?' Catarina said, shrugging.

'But we're on the fifth floor!' Olivier protested.

'So?' their friend said, pretending to be puzzled.

The Tangshan Tigers laughed. They should have been used to Catarina by now.

Climbing through a fifth-storey window was about as easy as walking up a flight of stairs for their agile friend.

Matt looked round Mr Wu's large, imposing office. There were sporting trophies on shelves all around the walls. A ceiling-high bookcase with leather-bound editions of classics, both European and Chinese. A state-of-the-art computer in matt black, with a flat, widescreen monitor sat atop a huge mahogany desk. The window Catarina had climbed in through was still open, the curtain flapping in the night breeze.

'Nice,' Shawn said, looking at the computer. 'A Stratoschwarz 6000 – top of the range. If Mr Wu's hiding any secrets about this tournament, this will be the place to find them.'

The Tangshan Tigers gathered round as Shawn flicked a switch. The computer came to life with a soft purr. An image of a silver-grey wolf staring up at a full moon filled the screen.

A dialogue box appeared beneath it. PLEASE ENTER PASSWORD.

'Hmm,' said Olivier. 'Could be a problem. Try his name?'

Shawn tapped it in.

INCORRECT PASSWORD ENTERED.

'How about just "password"?' said Catarina. 'Worth a try.'

'I doubt it,' said Shawn, but he tried anyway.

INCORRECT PASSWORD ENTERED.

'I don't like this,' said Shawn. 'These Stratoschwarzes – if you enter the incorrect password three times, they lock down. Like, totally freeze. Then we'll never get in. And Mr Wu will know someone's been tampering with it –'

'So we've got one more shot,' said Matt. 'What could it be?'

'He loves winning competitions,' said Olivier. 'What about "competition"? Or "tournament"?'

'Or "winning"?' said Catarina.

Matt snapped his fingers as a thought came to him. 'Try "victory",' he said.

'Yeah,' said Shawn. 'Victory – I like the sound of that. OK, let's do it!'

He typed the word in.

There was a breathless pause.

The screen lit up. Icons sprang into being all over the desktop.

The Tigers gave a restrained cheer.

'Next question,' said Olivier. 'What are we looking for, exactly?'

'I'm not sure,' Matt admitted. 'I'll know it when I see it.' He rubbed his chin. 'Try his emails?'

Shawn clicked on the email icon, then opened Wu's Inbox.

The four of them scanned the list of emails. But there was nothing you wouldn't expect to find – emails about academic matters, timetabling, school maintenance, budget reports, minutes of board meetings . . .

'Doesn't look like there's much –' began Catarina, but Olivier said '*Shush!*' and put his finger to his lips.

Footsteps came clumping by outside the office – one of the security guards doing his night rounds.

They stood in breathless silence. The footsteps passed by. They all breathed out in relief.

'Hey, that's weird,' said Matt, pointing at Mr Wu's Inbox.

'How come?' asked Catarina.

'The tournament's coming up in two days

– he's only just rescheduled it – and there's no mention of it anywhere in his recent emails. Unless – unless he's deleted all the references to Singapore!'

An electronic '*Bleep!*' from the computer made them all start.

'What's that?' said Matt.

'Oh, it's just a pop-up,' said Shawn. He pointed to an advertisement that had appeared on the screen, offering short-term loans, no questions asked. 'It's called spyware – it gets into your system and keeps pestering you with pop-up ads. Mr Wu's been a bit careless with his Internet surfing!'

'How do you mean, careless?' asked Matt, his interest awakening.

'Well, there are things you can do to protect yourself from getting infected with spyware, programmes to block it, but he obviously hasn't bothered. You tend to pick it up when you're surfing the net – especially on subscription sites. Sites you have to pay for, I mean.'

'Like what?' asked Olivier.

'Like low-rent shopping sites, or sites with games, or gambling . . .'

'How about we see Wu's Internet history over the last few days?' said Olivier. 'That might give us a clue.'

'No problem.'

The Tangshan Tigers crowded even closer around the computer as Shawn pulled down Wu's Internet history.

A list of websites filled the screen, flanked by brightly coloured ads of finance services, credit cards, loan agencies, betting companies, with graphics of dollar signs and moneybags and playing cards and roulette wheels.

Matt read the names of the sites visited aloud.

'Bets-Are-Us . . . Play-to-Win . . . Crazy Monkey Gambling Den . . . Double-or-Quits . . . Honest Johnson's Bookmakers . . . Win Win Win . . . Sporting Flutters . . . Better-Bets . . .'

The Tangshan Tigers gave a collective gasp.

'They're all gambling sites!' said Shawn.

'But what's he gambling on? Can you click on one of those sites, Shawn?' asked Olivier.

Shawn clicked on the first one. The website opened. A dialogue box said, WELOME, SILVER SHADOW.

'Must be the name he's using to gamble,' said Shawn. 'I guess he wouldn't want to be identified.'

The details of Mr Wu's bet came up: ten thousand dollars on the Beijing International Academy to beat Singapore, at evens.

'He's gambling on our match with Singapore!' exclaimed Matt.

'Evens – what does that mean?' asked Catarina.

'Means there's no favourite to win,' explained Shawn. 'Wu doubles his money if *we* win.'

'But why did he bet on so many different sites?' asked Olivier.

'It's called spread-betting,' Shawn explained. 'My uncle used to be crazy about betting before my aunt made him give it up – he explained it to me once. If Wu put all the money in one big lump in one place, the bookies might get scared and refuse to take it. Plus, if he did place a massive bet, he'd drive the odds down – they'd think he knew something, and Beijing would become favourites. By putting small or medium-sized bets on in lots of places he gets reasonable odds in all of them.'

'Ten thousand dollars?' said Matt. 'I don't call that small or medium-sized!'

'And he's done loads of them – where's he getting all the money?' said Catarina. 'It don't make sense.'

At that moment, an email alert came floating across the screen. It was from the People's Bank of China, Matt saw. He looked more closely, and drew in his breath.

'"Transfer of fifteen million yuan from Beijing International Academy account to personal account 11126573 confirmed",' he read. 'That's a million pounds! He's getting the money from the Academy and putting it into his own account!'

'He's gambling with the school's money!' said Shawn.

'I guess he's hoping to put it all back if he wins,' said Olivier. 'And pocket the profits, of course!'

'And if we lose . . . what then?' said Shawn. 'The school would have to close!'

'Even if we win, Wu would be in big trouble if this ever got out,' said Matt. 'He'd go to prison. And the reputation of the school would be ruined forever!'

'But how could Wu do this?' said Olivier. 'Say what you like about him, I always thought he was really proud of this school.'

'The guy's gone loco!' said Catarina, tapping the side of her head.

A sound outside made them stop talking. Footsteps again. *It must be the guard on his rounds again*, thought Matt, *nothing to worry about*.

The next second, they heard the key being jiggled in the door. Mr Wu must have come back!

The Tangshan Tigers stared at each other, frozen in alarm.

The jiggling continued. Thinking the door

was locked, Mr Wu was trying to unlock it, but he had only succeeded in relocking it. They heard him mutter in exasperation as the door refused to open. This gave them a few vital seconds.

'Quick!' whispered Catarina. 'Out the window!'

Shawn shut the computer down, scrambled over the window sill and disappeared. Olivier quickly followed.

Matt went next. The cold evening breeze ruffled his hair as he stepped out on to the narrow ledge beneath the window. He clung on tightly, not looking down. Shawn and Olivier crouched on the same ledge on the other side of the window.

Matt shifted along to make way for Catarina. But it was too late – Mr Wu had finally managed to unlock the door. Through the window Matt saw the handle turning.

Catarina was trapped. Her face was a picture of horror.

As the door opened, she sprang into action. She put one foot on the bookshelves near the door and nimbly, noiselessly hoisted herself up to ceiling-height. She braced herself against the corner formed by the wall, ceiling and the top of the bookcase. When Mr Wu entered the room, she was wedged above his head like a giant spider.

Matt held his breath.

'Catarina?' Olivier mouthed silently. He couldn't see in from where he was.

'She's OK,' Matt silently mouthed back. 'So far.'

Catarina was held in position only by the sheer force with which she pushed against the opposing surfaces; if she slackened off for a quarter of a second she'd come tumbling down. How long could she stay there?

Mr Wu bustled over to his desk. He pulled open the drawers, ferreting around for something. Matt heard him give a grunt of satisfaction as he pulled out a sheaf of papers. He closed the drawer – then he noticed the open window. He came over to close it. Matt shrank to one side; Shawn and Olivier did the same. Mr Wu only had to glance to one side or the other and the game would be up.

He stood for a moment, looking out and breathing in the night air. It seemed an endless moment to Matt.

At last, Wu closed the window and turned away.

Matt breathed again. He peered through the window and saw Mr Wu leaving the office, his head bowed over the papers he had picked up, oblivious to Catarina perched a metre and a half above his head.

Catarina's face was showing the strain –

her teeth were gritted together and her cheeks were crimson.

The door closed behind Wu.

Catarina dropped silently down. She breathed out with relief, shaking her dark hair away from her face. Then, grinning, she came over and opened the window.

'Hey, Catarina, that was fantastic!' said Matt as he climbed in.

'Yeah, fantastically painful!' said Catarina, rubbing her arm muscles.

Shawn and Olivier were now back in the room.

'What a night,' said Olivier. 'Never a dull moment round here, is there?'

'I don't think there's anything else we can do tonight, though,' said Matt. 'We found out the main thing – what's up with Mr Wu. Now we'd better get some rest – we've got a training session at six tomorrow, remember.'

'Yeah, if I haven't strained all my muscles clinging to the ceiling!' said Catarina.

The Tigers laughed.

'But what are we going to *do* about Wu?' asked Shawn.

'We'll think of something,' said Matt. 'We need to sleep on it.'

But Matt didn't think he'd sleep very much that night. There was too much to think about.

UNDERGROUND SURPRISE

'Good morning, everybody!' said Megan Walker.

She stood in the centre of the *kwoon*, wearing a bright red tracksuit. The squad gathered round her in a loose semicircle, some of them yawning and rubbing their eyes.

'This is way too early,' grumbled Carl. 'We should still be fast asleep in bed!' For once, Matt agreed with him.

'Nonsense,' said Miss Walker briskly. 'This is the best part of the day!' She looked fresh and wideawake, as though she'd already been up several hours.

But where was Chang?

Matt raised his hand. 'Excuse me, isn't this session with Chang Sifu? We thought –'

'I'm taking you on a field trip today – that's how come the early start. Chang Sifu doesn't need to accompany us.'

'Where are we going, Miss?' asked Lola.

'You'll see,' said Miss Walker. 'Follow me – the team bus is waiting outside.'

As they filed out after her, Matt beckoned to the other Tangshan Tigers.

'Anyone had any ideas?' asked Matt.

'About Mr Wu?' said Olivier. 'Could we tell one of the other teachers? Mr Figgis, maybe?'

'We'd have to admit we broke into Mr Wu's study and hacked into his computer,' Matt pointed out.

'What if we told Chang?' suggested Shawn. 'He'd be more understanding about that, I'm sure.'

'Maybe,' said Matt. The thought had already crossed his mind. But he wasn't entirely happy with it. 'I just sort of think Chang would prefer us to sort it ourselves. He's done that before; he wants us to stand on our own feet. If we went running to him for help it would be – like we'd failed.'

'Well, we *would* have failed!' said Catarina. 'And failing ain't what the Tangshan Tigers do, right?'

'Hurry up there!' called out Megan Walker from the front. 'You're lagging behind!'

Sighing, they caught up with the rest of the team and made their way outside to the bus.

'Here it is,' said Megan Walker. 'Champions' Gym.'

The squad gazed around at the impressive gymnasium they were standing in. It was ultramodern, ultrastylish – *and must cost a fortune to belong to*, thought Matt. Situated in the very centre of Beijing, it was a huge building; from where Matt stood, he could see a roomful of people working out on weights, rowing machines and running machines. A little further off, some gymnasts were doing vaulting and parallel-bar exercises; at the far end of the sports hall, so far away the players looked tiny, a game of volleyball was in progress.

The martial arts area was much larger than the *kwoon* at the Academy, with several full-sized combat mats. Some men in combat attire were warming up on the mat next to the one where Megan Walker had gathered the Beijing squad.

'Wow!' said Shawn. 'This is quite something!'

'Glad it meets with your approval,' said Megan Walker. 'This is where I do my martial arts training.'

'You do martial arts?' said Carl incredulously. He hadn't taken to Megan Walker, Matt could tell.

'Yes – why?'

Carl shrugged. 'Just can't imagine you on the mat, that's all.'

Without turning or repositioning herself, Megan suddenly shot out her leg in a high kick directed at Carl's face.

Her foot came to a stop one millimetre away from Carl's nose.

Carl jumped back – although his jump would have been too late had Megan's kick really been intended to connect. 'Hey! What the –'

'Didn't expect that, did you? Never underestimate a potential opponent,' said

Megan. 'I could put out a man's eye with my big toe.'

There was a slight gasp from the squad at this. Matt could hardly believe what he'd just heard. Megan Walker coughed. 'Only if I wanted to, of course,' she added hastily. 'Don't worry, I won't do it to you guys.'

There was a nervous silence.

How on earth does Mr Wu know someone like this? Matt wondered.

'Anyway,' Megan resumed, 'I've brought you here today to watch some expert martial artists in action – to see what it looks like when it's done properly.'

Matt felt a stir of resentment on Chang Sifu's behalf. Was she saying Chang wasn't an expert?

'Oh, and by the way,' said Megan, 'have you all been watching those DVDs I gave you?'

A few of the team said they had. Matt nodded. He had glanced at the DVD briefly last night. It was full of martial arts sequences, intercut with serious-faced people staring at the camera and saying things like, 'Winning isn't everything; it's the only thing,' and 'Show me a good loser and I'll show you a loser!' The idea seemed to be that you must want to win at all costs and do everything in your power to destabilize and humiliate your opponents. It was very different from Chang Sifu's philosophy of honour in combat.

'Good. Keep watching 'em,' said Megan. 'You gotta develop that hunger to win at all costs – if you can blend that with the kind of skill levels you'll see here today, you'll be unbeatable!'

She motioned the squad to sit down at the side of the combat arena. Matt felt a flicker of excitement – he loved watching martial arts experts at work.

Two men in martial arts suits took to the mat. They were both tall, over six foot, and broad and burly in proportion. One was black, the other white. Matt was good at assessing a fighter's capabilities from his or her appearance – he could tell just by looking at these two that they knew what they were doing. They were obviously super-fit – their bodies looked sharply defined and they carried themselves confidently.

They faced each other and bowed.

Matt was expecting a display of judo, or ju-jitsu, or wrestling. The two men were solid and burly, physically suited to the grappling, holding, take-down styles of fighting.

The bout began when the black fighter took a flying leap, turned round 360 degrees in mid-air, and launched a kick at his opponent's head. His opponent dived *under* the kick, rolled, bounced up and threw out a backwards kick that the black fighter jumped *over*.

Matt was dazzled. The two men performed somersaults, handsprings, cartwheels and moves that seemed to belong as much to ballet as to martial arts. At the same time they were throwing serious punches and kicks from every conceivable angle. Matt had never seen fighting that looked so full of power, yet at the same time so graceful.

'It's fantastic!' he said to Catarina, who was sitting beside him.

'It's *capoeira*,' said Catarina. 'I should know – that's my martial art! But I dunno if I'll ever be able to do it like this. These guys are something else!'

'I don't know how they do it,' said Matt.

'They must weigh fifteen stone each, but they're bouncing around like they weigh nothing at all!'

'That's right,' said Megan Walker, who was standing behind Matt. 'It's partly due to this gym – it's got a specially sprung floor. Feel it. Like this.' She bounced up and down on the balls of her feet. Matt followed suit. The floor felt springy – it gave very slightly beneath the feet, then bounced back.

The rest of the squad were also trying it. 'Hey!' said Lola. 'It's like being on a trampoline!'

'Well, kind of,' said Megan. 'That's because this gym is built over a cavity – a hole dug out of the Beijing earth. Beneath the floor there's just an empty old cave. This specially sprung floor gives the fighters an extra bit of bounce – it also softens the impact of a fall.'

Wow, thought Matt. *An empty cave right*

underneath busy, bustling Beijing. This is an amazing city!

'But there's more to the performance of these guys than just a bouncy floor,' Megan went on. 'It's down to dedication – you don't get near that level of skill without constant practice. These guys train six hours a day; that's why they're among the best in the world. And if you ever hope to get anywhere near that level, your martial art has to be the most important thing in life for you. The *only* thing in life.'

Matt shared a look with the other Tangshan Tigers. He loved martial arts, but didn't think he was capable of devoting his whole life to it. There were other important things too – like friendship and fun. And, if you happened to be a Tangshan Tiger, catching criminals.

He could see that the others were thinking

the same thing. Shawn frowned slightly, Olivier shook his head, and Catarina stuck out her lower lip.

Matt returned his attention to the exhibition bout. It was certainly worth watching. The tempo of the fight increased all the time. The white fighter performed a somersault and lashed out with a kick as he came down; the black fighter caught his foot and flipped him. He performed a back somersault. The black fighter cartwheeled towards him and threw a three-punch combination as he was still rising; the white fighter parried all three punches then swung a roundhouse kick at his opponent; the black fighter jumped over it, spun and threw a snap kick from the hip . . .

The fight ended when they caught each other simultaneously with a kick to the jaw. They both fell over, lay flat on their backs for a second, then flipped themselves upright again by a spectacular backward roll.

They bowed to one another and walked off the mat.

The Beijing squad laughed and clapped. *That last move must have been rehearsed*, Matt thought. But it had been so skilfully done you had to admire it. In a real fight, either of these men would be an opponent to fear.

'Glad you liked it,' said Megan as the applause subsided. 'You see what you can achieve if you dedicate your life to it? Now, we're going to watch some other exhibitions from different martial arts disciplines – just stay put for a moment while I go and sort that out.'

She walked over to the other side of the combat arena and was soon in conversation with some of the white-suited athletes there.

'What do you think?' asked Matt.

'Impressive stuff,' said Shawn. 'More fun than being in double maths. But it won't be much help if we have to retake our exams.'

The gym was quieter now the exhibition bout had finished. Matt heard the low hum of the running machines, the distant click of the rowing machines, the odd shout from the volleyball game at the far end, and not much else. Except, somewhere, there was a strange muted cry. It came and went, mingling with the other sounds echoing around the sports hall – yet it seemed to be coming from somewhere else.

It didn't sound like a cry of exertion or frustration. It sounded more like . . . An icy chill ran through Matt as he realized it sounded like a cry of distress.

A call for help.

'Did you hear that?' he whispered urgently to his friends.

'No – what?' said Olivier.

Again came the cry – quiet, muffled, but full of desperation.

'There!' said Matt.

'Yes – I heard it that time,' said Olivier.

'Someone's in trouble,' said Catarina.

'But where's it coming from?' said Matt.

'Sounded like it came from under the floor,' said Shawn.

They listened again. But the cry for help had stopped.

'It could be coming from under the floor,' said Olivier slowly. 'The cavity she mentioned, remember?'

'You reckon someone's trapped down there?' asked Catarina.

'Sounds pretty weird, I admit,' said Olivier. 'But we've come across some pretty weird stuff before. And we did all hear it. I think we should check it out.'

'I'll come with you,' said Matt.

'Let's all go!' said Catarina.

'No – if we do that, Walker will wonder where we've gone.' Some instinct warned Matt not to let Megan Walker in on this. 'You two stay here, and if she asks, tell her we've gone to the toilet.'

'OK,' said Shawn. 'Here, you may need this.' He handed Matt his Universal Key. 'I put a nitrogen refill in this morning, just in case – good job I did!'

'What are you guys whispering about?' asked Carl, turning to stare at them.

'Nothing,' said Olivier. 'Well, we were just chatting about Megan Walker, saying she's a bit of a dark horse and –'

'She'd never have got me with that kick,' said Carl. 'I would have dodged if it had been about to hit me.'

No one answered. *If it makes Carl happier*

to think that, thought Matt, *well, let him*.

He and Olivier stole away towards the exit while Megan Walker's back was still turned. Once out of the sports hall, there was a foyer that led to the way out, or to the changing rooms, or to a downward staircase that was not signposted.

Matt and Olivier took the staircase.

The steps went down in a steep spiral, lit by naked electric bulbs at intervals along the rough, unpainted brickwork.

'Pretty different to upstairs, isn't it?' said Olivier.

It got colder the further down they went. They were both shivering when they reached the bottom of the staircase and came up against a black iron door.

Matt tried the handle. Locked.

'Thank goodness for Shawn's Universal Key!' said Matt.

He took the key, inserted it into the lock and pressed the bulb. Water squirted into the keyhole, then there was a click and a hiss as the liquid nitrogen was released. A moment later, a solid ice key had formed, which exactly fitted the interior of the lock. Matt turned it, and the door swung open with a creak.

A dark passageway was revealed. The floor was of hard, compacted earth. Cobwebs hung from the ceiling. The only light came from a glimmer further down the passage, where the walls curved away out of sight. It looked creepy, to say the least.

'After you,' said Olivier.

'Well, that's very kind of you, Olivier,' said Matt.

He stepped into the passage. Olivier joined him. Together they cautiously made their way forward.

Their steps slowed as they approached the bend. The light shone more brightly, but they still couldn't see what was round the corner. *It could be anything*, thought Matt. *A gang's headquarters, a torture chamber . . .*

At that moment, they heard the cry again – the same desolate, strangled cry they'd heard upstairs, but much closer.

Matt and Olivier looked at each other.

'There's no turning back now,' said Matt. 'We're here, we've got to –'

'I know,' said Olivier. 'Let's do it.'

They rounded the bend – and both gasped in amazement.

They were in a large, bowl-shaped chamber. The ceiling was high, some twenty metres above. Lamps were hung around the walls.

In the centre, a figure sat tied to a chair. The figure was gagged. At the sight of

Matt and Olivier, he began to writhe furiously, uttering more of those strangled cries.

The face was half covered by the gag, and shiny with sweat. But they still had no difficulty in recognizing him . . .

'Mr Wu?' said Matt.

A CLEAN SWEEP

'Unnh – urrrhh – urrghmpphh!' exclaimed their principal.

'Here, let's get that off you!' said Olivier. Mr Wu had already succeeded in working loose a corner of the gag. Olivier tore the rest away. It had been affixed with sticky tape and Mr Wu yelped in pain as it tugged at his skin.

'Sorry, sir.'

'Please be careful, there is no excuse for –' began Mr Wu in his usual loud, pompous manner. But then he stopped. He breathed deeply a few times. 'I should – I must thank you,' he said more quietly. 'Thank you most sincerely. For rescuing me. I began to wonder how long I should be imprisoned down here.'

'How long have you been here, sir?' asked Matt.

'Difficult to tell,' said Mr Wu, shaking his head. 'There are no clocks. You must have a better idea than me – how long since I was missed at school?'

'Well, you haven't exactly been missed,' said Matt carefully. 'I mean, there's someone there in your place. Someone who looks like you.'

'An impostor?' shrieked Mr Wu.

'Er, well, yeah,' said Matt. Now that he looked closely at the real Wu, he wondered how he had ever been deceived by the fake one. The impostor did bear a strong resemblance to Mr Wu – he was the same age and build, had a similar nose and the same-shaped mouth, the same pointed teeth. But he wasn't identical – Matt could see now that there was a difference about the eyes, and Mr Wu's complexion was very slightly darker. *That's why the other guy wore make-up*, he realized. But even more telling than the physical differences were the differences of character. Matt should have guessed that it wasn't the real Mr Wu shouting at people, humiliating Mrs Tyler, being openly rude to Chang, gambling away the school's money. Mr Wu was vain and pompous, but he was a gentleman, not a bully or a crook.

Olivier was busy untying Mr Wu's bonds. 'How were you captured, sir?' he asked. 'And who did it?'

'I do not know,' said Mr Wu. 'I had just

left the bank and someone grabbed me from behind and I was pushed into a car. They put a bag over my head, I did not see who did it. But I thought I heard a woman's voice.'

'A woman's voice?' Matt immediately wondered if their new motivational trainer had anything to do with it. It couldn't be a coincidence that she'd joined the squad at the same time that Mr Wu disappeared. And that he was held captive under the gym that she belonged to. 'Could it have been Megan Walker?' he said.

'Who?' said Mr Wu.

'The new motivational coach.'

'What motivational coach?'

'We can explain all that later,' said Olivier. 'We need to get out of here now, get you back to the school, call the police and have the impostor arrested −'

'No!' said Mr Wu. 'I do not want scandal. It would damage the school's reputation.'

'Do you mean you want to just go back and confront him privately?' said Matt. 'Let him slip away and –'

'No!' said Mr Wu. 'He must be brought to justice!'

'Then how –' began Olivier.

'We must proceed with caution,' said Mr Wu. 'Collect evidence to charge him. Discreetly, of course.' He paused in thought, rubbing the side of his cheek where the gag had left a red mark. 'The difficulty is, if I show my face in the school I shall be recognized and the impostor will take flight.'

'Not if you were in disguise!' said Matt. 'Suppose we disguised you as, say, a cleaner . . .'

'A cleaner?' said Mr Wu in distaste.

'That's a great idea!' said Olivier. 'Matt, if

you went back to the school with Mr Wu
you could get hold of a cleaner's uniform
and smuggle him in.'

'Yeah, but Walker will wonder where I am.'

'That's OK,' said Olivier. 'I'll think of a
story for her. Let's see, if I say you have
a really embarrassing problem – one that's
made you want to rush back to the school
alone without seeing anyone . . .?'

'Like what?' said Matt uneasily. He wasn't
sure he liked where this was going.

'What's the one illness no one would ever
dare to ask about?' Olivier said. Mr Wu
frowned in confusion, looking from Matt to
Olivier and back again.

'Er . . .' Matt felt the blood drain from his
face. 'Not – diarrhoea?'

'Yup. That's it,' said Olivier, grinning. 'Toilet
trouble. I'll say it's really bad and you're
having trouble holding it in –'

'OK, shut up, that's enough!' said Matt. He shook his head ruefully. 'I guess there's not much choice, is there?'

The things he had to do for the Tangshan Tigers.

'Here you are, sir,' said Matt, handing over a dark blue set of cleaner's overalls. He had borrowed a spare set from the cleaners' cubbyhole on the ground floor.

Mr Wu was standing in his vest, pants and socks behind a bush in the Academy gardens. 'Hurry, give them quickly!' His arm came snaking out through the leaves and grabbed the overalls. The bush rustled and shook as he put them on.

'These overalls are a very poor fit,' he said bitterly. 'Baggy and shapeless. Also the fabric is coarse and of poor quality.'

'It's only for the time being,' said Matt.

'I must think about changing suppliers,' said Mr Wu. 'A school with the prestige of the Beijing International Academy should have smarter cleaners. I have taken too little care of this.'

'You'd better put this on, sir,' said Matt, handing Mr Wu a peaked cleaner's cap.

Mr Wu emerged from the bush, with the cap jammed low over his face. 'How do I look?'

'Perfect,' said Matt, trying to suppress a grin at the sight of the usually dapper Mr Wu in a scruffy old boiler suit. 'All you need's a broom!'

'I do not propose to do any sweeping!' said Mr Wu sharply. 'Where can I put my suit?'

'In here,' said Matt, holding out the plastic bag he'd brought the overalls in.

'But it will get crumpled,' said Mr Wu.

'You can have it cleaned and pressed,' said

Matt. 'Once we've sorted the impostor out.'

'I suppose there is no help for it,' said Mr Wu, carefully pushing his tailored suit into the carrier bag. 'You will be sure to hang it up, won't you?'

'Of course,' promised Matt. 'I'll hang it in my wardrobe.'

'Now what happens next?' asked Mr Wu. 'Where do I go in my – disguise?' He plucked at the rough material of the overalls.

'I've phoned my friends Shawn, Olivier and Catarina,' said Matt. There was no need to tell Mr Wu about the Tangshan Tigers, of course. 'They'll be here in a minute and we'll find somewhere you can lie low.'

'And then?'

'And then we'll make a plan.'

Matt heard a low whistle and turned to see the other Tigers coming towards them, skirting the wall of the school building.

'Hey, great disguise, sir,' said Catarina. 'You look like Super Mario!'

'Who? I have not the honour of his acquaintance.'

'We need to find somewhere Mr Wu can hide out,' said Matt. 'Any ideas?'

'One of the cleaners' storerooms,' said Olivier swiftly. 'They're kept locked, so no one's going to come blundering in.'

'A storeroom?' said Mr Wu unhappily.

He allowed himself to be led away by the Tangshan Tigers. Catarina went into the school by the front entrance and opened one of the back doors for them.

They hurried through the corridors and found a storeroom tucked away in a shadowy recess, for which Mr Wu fortunately had a spare key in his suit pocket.

'Here we are then!' said Matt.

Mr Wu looked around at the shelves of

floor polish, bottles of bleach and other cleaning products.

'I had no idea the cleaners' supplies were so low,' he observed. 'I must order a stock-take at once!'

'Yes, but not yet,' said Matt. 'We need to sort this situation out first.'

Mr Wu sighed. 'Perhaps I should just contact the police straight away,' he said. 'If only I knew what the impostor's game was –'

'But we do know,' said Matt. He explained about the tournament and the fake Wu's gambling. He took care not to mention such minor details as sneaking into the Principal's office. Mr Wu was fortunately too shocked to ask any awkward questions.

'You mean – the tournament has been brought forward?' said Mr Wu, when Matt had finished.

'Yes,' said Shawn. 'In fact, it's tomorrow.'

'Then we cannot expose the impostor now!' said Mr Wu. His face was a picture of dismay. 'If we do, there is no way of avoiding the visiting Singapore School finding out about it! Then the scandal will be all over Asia – all over the world!'

'But what's the alternative?' said Olivier. 'You don't want to stay *here* forever?'

'No – only until after the tournament. But I cannot risk exposure – I would lose face, do you understand?' He was short of breath and a bright red spot had appeared on each of his cheeks.

'OK,' said Matt. 'We'll do what we can. Leave it with us. We'd better get you some food if you're going to be hiding in here for a while.'

Catarina ran to the Academy tuck shop – a large glittering store with foods, snacks and treats from every country in the world. She

came back with a sandwich, some fruit and a
bottle of water.

'Thank you,' said Mr Wu. 'And I can rely
on you to – to keep quiet about this, and
also find a way to stop the impostor's plans?'

'Sure,' said Matt. 'We'll do our best, sir.'

Mr Wu nodded, a glimmer of his usual
self-satisfaction returning. 'I see I have trained
you well. Adaptability and quick thinking.
You are a credit to my Academy!'

Mr Wu sat on a little three-legged stool
and waved them away.

Matt and the rest of the Tigers shared a
secret glance and rolled their eyes.

'That's definitely the real Mr Wu,'
whispered Matt as they left the storeroom.
'No one else takes as much credit for other
people's efforts as he does.'

Matt turned for one last look at Mr Wu.
He was surrounded by shelves of cleaning

products, in his baggy boiler suit. It was difficult not to smile at the sight. But Matt managed to keep a straight face.

'Do not forget to hang up my suit!' called out Mr Wu.

'He's left us with a pretty tricky problemo,' said Catarina, sitting on the bed with her chin in her hands. They had met up in Shawn and Olivier's room after supper. 'It looks like we either try and win the tournament – so Fake-Wu wins a fortune, and if we're not careful, runs outta here with it! Or – we throw the tournament, give up our perfect record and let the squad down.'

'And our Sifu,' Matt pointed out.

Catarina frowned. Matt could tell neither option appealed to her. Or to any of the Tangshan Tigers.

'Or we just go to the police!' said Olivier, stretching out his legs and putting his hands behind his head. 'I don't see why Mr Wu's got such a problem with that.'

'It's all about saving face,' said Shawn. 'He's supposed to be the Principal, the authority figure. If it got out that he'd been kidnapped and impersonated, he'd be totally shamed. He'd have to resign. And it would be bad news for the reputation of the Academy. Believe me, this sort of stuff is taken very seriously here.'

'So we have to help him hush it up,' said Matt slowly. He began to feel more sympathetic to Mr Wu. He had been thinking of Wu as a figure of fun. But in his efforts to save face there was a kind of dignity too.

'So that means we can't accuse him until after the Singapore guys have gone,' said

Catarina. 'It comes back to that first choice: do we throw the contest or not?' She flung herself on to the bed.

'We can't throw the contest!' said Matt, leaning forward in his chair. 'That would go against everything Chang Sifu's ever taught us. You have to strive to be as good as you can. It makes a mockery of the whole thing if we lose on purpose.'

'So we try to win, and risk letting Fake-Wu get away with several million dollars?' said Shawn. 'He won't hang around once the tournament's finished, you can bet!'

Matt shook his head. 'No. I don't think we should do that either.'

'Unfortunately, that leaves us with no choices at all,' said Olivier dryly.

'I'm not so sure,' said Matt. 'Think about what Chang has taught us. Never give up. There's always another way, he says. Be flexible, be adaptable. If an opponent blocks one move, try another, remember?'

'Yeah, but – how does that work here?' said Olivier. 'We either try to win or we don't – there aren't any other options!'

'What if it isn't an either-or choice?' said Matt. 'What if we try to win the tournament AND stop the impostor winning his bets?'

'Yeah, dream-ticket,' said Olivier. 'But how?'

'This is what I'm thinking,' said Matt. He looked at the three expectant faces before him. 'Shawn – do you think you could hack into the Fake-Wu's gambling accounts?'

'Sure thing,' Shawn pulled his BlackBerry from his pocket. In a few moments, he had pulled up all the Silver Shadow's gambling accounts. He held up the BlackBerry for the others to see.

'That's great!' said Matt. 'So – could you

wipe out all the bets he's laid? Delete them?'

Shawn shook his head regretfully. 'Not unless he enters these sites himself. Until he gives his authorization to add bets, the site will be read-only.'

'But if he makes new bets?'

'If I'm online at the same time, yeah, I probably could find a way to override what he's doing.'

'But will he make any more bets?' asked Olivier.

'I'd say he will,' said Shawn, sitting up straight. 'He'll place more bets on the day – the odds will change after each bout, you see, and he's bound to stake more money. I bet he brings his laptop to the tournament!'

'But won't that look funny, if he's paying more attention to his laptop than the action?' said Catarina.

'What does he care?' said Shawn. 'He'll be away straight after the tournament.'

'Somehow we've got to combat everything he does while we're fighting Singapore,' said Matt. 'It's going to be tricky, but Chang has always taught us to keep our focus, no matter what the distraction. This is our chance to put that into action!'

'Someone's bound to notice if we're all hunched over a laptop, though,' said Olivier. 'The Principal could get away with that, but not us.'

'No worries,' said Shawn. 'The BlackBerry will do just fine. It's small enough to hide easily, but it's got all the software to track the Fake-Wu on the Internet. I'll stalk him and rub out his bets as he places them!'

'You know, Shawn, you worry me – if you put your mind to it, you could be the world's greatest criminal mastermind!' joked Catarina, slapping him on the shoulder.

'No thanks – I'd rather *catch* criminals than *be* one!' said Shawn.

'So that's the plan,' said Matt, rising to his feet. 'Agreed?'

'Agreed!' cried his friends. They high-fived each other.

Matt and Catarina headed back to their rooms. They would need a good night's rest if they were to be fresh for the tasks ahead of them tomorrow.

As he laid his head on the pillow, Matt thought of Mr Wu in the storeroom. He hoped the Principal would get a good night's sleep too. If he didn't, the Tangshan Tigers would never hear the end of it.

TIMEOUT

'How are you, sir?' asked Matt.

He and the other Tigers had gone to the storeroom to check on Mr Wu and take him some breakfast. It was the day of the tournament and the Academy was buzzing with excitement. The Singapore team had already arrived in their gleaming team bus – the tournament was due to start at midday.

'I have been keeping busy,' said Mr Wu.

He certainly had. Matt saw that he had rearranged all the cleaning products in straight lines on the shelves and had pinned on the wall a list, in tiny, super-neat handwriting, of all the products that were running low and needed re-ordering.

'It looks really nice, sir,' said Catarina.

'Yes, it is an improvement, isn't it?' said Mr Wu proudly. Then his expression became serious. 'But let us turn to more urgent matters. The impostor – he is still here? He doesn't suspect?'

'Yeah, he's here,' said Shawn. The Fake-Wu had greeted the Singapore team when they arrived and appeared to be in a state of high excitement.

'I thought he might have fled when news of my escape came to him. But it is good that he has not,' said Mr Wu.

'With so much money at stake, he must have decided to tough it out,' said Matt. 'He's probably hoping that you'd be so keen to avoid the scandal, you wouldn't expose him while the visiting team was here – and he'll take the first opportunity to get away afterwards.'

Which he'd have a fair chance of pulling off, if the Tangshan Tigers weren't around, Matt thought.

'But he will not get away!' said Mr Wu. 'I will confront him – confound him – destroy the evil impostor!'

'Yes, but remember to stay put here until we tell you the coast is clear, after the tournament,' said Olivier. 'Because if anyone sees the two of you together, they'll know at once –'

'Of course, of course, I do not need to be told this!' said Mr Wu. 'You will please let me know when it is safe to come out.'

'Sure thing, sir,' said Shawn.

'It is – very good of you to help in this way,' said Mr Wu. He spoke with some effort, as though not used to thanking people. *But still*, thought Matt, *he did it*. 'It is almost like having a team of special crime-fighters working for me – what a strange idea!'

'Crazy!' said Catarina.

The Tangshan Tigers laughed, exchanging glances.

If only Mr Wu knew.

The atmosphere in the changing room was tense. The Beijing team – Matt, Catarina, Olivier, Shawn, Carl, Wolfgang, Paolo, Andrei, Jahmal, Abdul and Lola, whom Chang had made captain for this match – sat on the polished wooden benches, already changed into their martial arts gear. Chang Sifu was with them; his presence made Matt feel calmer, more reassured. Chang gave Lola a slight nod, as though indicating she should speak to the team.

'Well, guys, we haven't had much preparation

for this,' said Lola. 'But neither have they. And we have the home advantage. They are a tough team, but I think we can do it!'

What Lola didn't know, thought Matt, was that the Tangshan Tigers had to try and win an electronic battle with Fake-Wu at the same time. Which made things difficult.

'Anyway if we don't win it's so not our fault,' said Carl petulantly. 'If I lose today it shouldn't count!'

'It *will* count, I'm afraid,' said Lola. 'So try not to lose!'

'We only got back from England three days ago, I'm still jet-lagged, we've had a whole day of exams, plus all that extra training with that motivational maniac –'

'Where is Megan Walker, anyway?' asked Matt suddenly.

'She is not here today,' said Chang. 'Has not arrived.'

'Ah,' said Matt softly. A look passed between him and the Tigers. Of course it made sense that Megan Walker had not turned up – if she was in on the plot, she'd have hightailed it away as soon as she discovered Wu was missing. It was possible that she hadn't even told the Fake-Wu. Matt hoped not – that would mean he still didn't know about the real Wu's escape.

But there was no more time to think about this. The electronic twang of the *guzheng* sounded through the *kwoon*.

'The tournament will commence in five minutes!' The voice of the Fake-Wu came over the tannoy. 'Please take your seats.'

'Got the team sheet here,' announced Lola. 'Matt, you're gonna be up first . . .'

Matt was getting to be a veteran of tournaments now – but he still felt the excitement of the occasion as strongly as the first ever time.

The *kwoon* was filled with spectators who broke into applause as soon as the Beijing team made its appearance. They were nearly all Beijing students, of course, and delighted at having the unexpected time off lessons to watch a martial arts contest. Johnny, recovered from his flu, was sitting in the front row and gave Matt a big thumbs-up sign.

On one side of the square combat mat was the judges' table, behind which three stern-looking judges sat.

On the opposite side of the mat to the Beijing squad was the Singapore team. They were dressed in cool, shiny red uniforms. They looked fit and athletic as far as physique went, but their faces were tired. Not only had they had to prepare for this in a hurry, just like Beijing, but they had also endured a five-hour flight on top of that. They scowled bad-temperedly at the BIA team – *and no wonder*, thought Matt.

Their coach didn't look in the best of tempers either. He was a middle-aged European with a broad chest and a little dark beard. When Master Chang went over to greet him, he bowed slightly, but did not shake Chang's outstretched hand. *He must think it was Chang's decision to bring the match forward*, thought Matt.

Chang did not appear to take this personally. He nodded gently and moved away.

Fake-Wu, meanwhile, appeared to be in a state of hyper-excitement. He couldn't keep still. He kept striding around the hall. He came up to the Beijing squad, clenched both fists and barked hoarsely, 'C'mon! You can do it!'

His cheeks were flushed, his eyes were bulging – and his behaviour so unlike the real Mr Wu's that the Beijing team stared in amazement.

Fake-Wu moved over to where the judges sat and picked up the microphone from their table.

'I would like to welcome you all to this auspicious occasion. It is going to be a GREAT contest. All praise to Singapore Intercontinental School for putting their unbeaten record on the line – I can assure you it is at great RISK today,' he said, smiling unpleasantly at the Singapore coach. 'My team are highly trained and motivated, at the top of their game!' He turned and pumped his fist at the Beijing team. 'Who's the best? What do we say? The answer is the BIA!'

A blast of a military march came over the tannoy. Matt recognized it as the soundtrack to Megan's motivational DVD. It was so loud that half the spectators put their hands over their ears. Fake-Wu pumped his fist in the air in time to the music, gesturing at the BIA team to do the same.

None of them did.

Matt felt himself grow hot with embarrassment. He could sense Catarina squirming uncomfortably beside him. The Singapore coach was stony-faced. *He must think he's come to a madhouse*, thought Matt.

He glanced at Chang Sifu. Chang was standing with his hands by his sides, gazing intently at the impostor. Something in his gaze made Matt wonder. *Does he know? If he knows, why doesn't he say anything?*

The music stopped, thankfully.

'Without further ado, let's get on with the action!' said Fake-Wu.

He sat down behind the judges. He settled

his laptop on his knees. Matt watched him closely. He jumped as one of the judges called his name out.

'Matt James versus Gianni Barenza!'

'Go on, Matt!' called Lola. 'Show them what you can do!'

Matt made his way out to the middle, his head buzzing. His opponent was short, squat and muscular. Low centre of gravity. He looked like a typical take-down fighter – a judo or ju-jitsu fighter.

They faced each other on the mat.

'The winner is the first to three points, or whoever is in the lead after three minutes,' the judge announced.

The arena went quiet.

They bowed.

Focus, Matt told himself. *Like Chang's always taught us. Shut out all distractions . . .*

At that moment, there was a very slight

hum as Fake-Wu switched on his laptop. Matt couldn't help glancing round at him and –

Oooof!

Gianni Barenza crashed into his midriff like a tank in fourth gear.

Matt was propelled backwards. He was just able to plant his feet and save himself from going over, but he kept being driven back. He was unable to break free and find the space to employ his trademark kicks and punches.

Barenza was trying to hook his leg behind Matt's and throw him. Matt knew some of the techniques of close-quarter fighting – Chang had always trained them to be versatile, to use both stand-up and take-down styles – and defended as well as he could. But this wasn't his style of fighting. He was only able to postpone the moment when Barenza sent him over.

A point to Barenza!

Matt started to roll before he hit the floor. If Barenza managed to pin him, that would be another two points against him and he'd have lost his bout.

Barenza landed on top, but Matt's rolling motion had put him off-balance. He scrabbled for Matt's arm, but Matt avoided the hold, grabbed Barenza's own arm and used it as a lever to pull himself up.

'Go on, Matt!' called Lola. 'Focus!'

Barenza's team were calling out too, but Matt shut them out. He had to focus. Ignore Fake-Wu on his laptop. That was part of the same battle, but Shawn was dealing with it; Matt's part had to be played out here in the arena.

Suddenly his head felt clearer. He felt lighter on his feet. He was going to fight on his own terms – he was ready to hit

Barenza with every tae kwon-do move he possessed.

Barenza was up and charging at him again.

Matt shaped to perform a crescent kick, but this wasn't his real counter-attack, merely a feint to initiate a response. Sure enough, Barenza's hands went up to defend. Matt rotated sideways, away from Barenza, while drawing his knee towards himself. Barenza was bamboozled – his hands were still up, but the promised crescent kick had faded away and Matt seemed to be in retreat. Then Matt kicked backwards, hard – a piercing side-kick that caught Barenza in the ribs.

One point all.

Cheers from the Beijing supporters!

The fighters stood off, breathing hard. Before Barenza could try another rush attack, Matt came towards him, leading with both hands. He closed the gap between them – too short for a kick, the obvious threat was from his jabbing fists.

Again, Barenza's hands came up to defend against punches. He came forward himself, looking to block then get in close and grapple.

Matt leapt backwards and rotated in mid-air, flinging out a reverse kick as hard as he could.

The result was spectacular. The kick connected perfectly and knocked Barenza clean over.

Under the competition rules, a kick or punch that connected cleanly with a target area scored a single point; but a kick or punch that resulted in a knock-down scored two.

'James wins by three points to one,' announced the judge. 'Overall score, Beijing one, Singapore nil.'

Matt went back to his team-mates with the crowd's applause ringing in his ears. But he had no time to savour his triumph. He needed to know how Shawn was doing in the cyber-battle against Fake-Wu.

Shawn was holding his BlackBerry in one hand, shielding it with the other. Catarina and Olivier sat next to him. They all grinned at Matt's approach, and Shawn gave a quick thumbs-up.

'It's working?' whispered Matt.

'Got him on the first site,' said Shawn. 'Wiped it out.'

'Look at him!' said Olivier. 'He doesn't understand it −'

'And he doesn't like it!' added Catarina.

Matt looked across at Fake-Wu. He was staring at his laptop in bafflement and anger, as though it had just bitten him.

'He'll try another gambling site in a

minute,' said Shawn. 'And I'll get him there too!'

'Next bout, Shawn Hung versus Junior Mackenzie.'

Catarina pointed at Shawn's BlackBerry. 'What do we do with this while you're out there?'

'It's kinda complicated –'

'Is there anything we can do to help?' asked Matt.

'You better get out there, Shawn,' said Lola.

Shawn's opponent was already waiting on the mat.

'I gotta go,' said Shawn. 'Don't worry, I'll be back as soon as I can.'

He went to face Mackenzie: a tall, loose-limbed, gangling boy.

Mackenzie went into action quickly. He was a *karateka* and scored with his first attack, hitting Shawn with a side-kick to the thigh.

Matt felt worried. The boy was fast, but so was Shawn – he shouldn't have allowed himself to be caught so easily.

The fighters circled each other warily. Shawn made no move to attack.

Then Mackenzie came in again with a combination of hand-strikes. Shawn blocked – Mackenzie's guard was momentarily down and Shawn had a clear opportunity to move in and try for a throw, or hold.

'Go on, Shawn!' shouted Matt.

But Shawn didn't go for the opportunity. He backed off – and now, once again, it was Mackenzie on the attack.

Suddenly Matt realized what Shawn was doing. *I'll be back as soon as I can*, he'd said. He was deliberately throwing the match, so he could get back to the cyber-battle on his BlackBerry as soon as possible!

Matt glanced over at the Fake-Wu. He was

tapping away on his laptop contentedly, no longer confused – he wasn't even watching the fight.

A shout went up. Matt looked back at the action. Shawn was rubbing his side – Mackenzie must have caught him again.

If Mackenzie scored one more point, it would be the end of the bout.

'He's throwing the fight!' Matt whispered to Catarina and Olivier. 'What are we going to do?'

'We could ask for a timeout,' murmured Olivier. 'It's in the rules.'

Matt tugged at Lola's sleeve. 'Can we call a timeout?'

'Just because your mate's losing!' sneered Carl. 'I didn't notice anyone calling a timeout last time I was down in a bout!'

'This is different!' said Matt.

'Yeah, right.'

'Sifu?' said Lola. 'Can I call a timeout?'

Chang inclined his head.

Lola leapt to her feet and shouted in an unexpectedly loud voice for such a small person, 'Timeout!'

An abrupt silence fell. Shawn looked round at his team in surprise. Mackenzie, who had been about to launch his third and probably final attack, looked helplessly at his coach, who gave an angry shrug. *He must think we're really bad sports*, thought Matt. A pity, but it couldn't be helped.

Even Fake-Wu stopped tapping on his laptop and looked up, nonplussed.

'Ninety seconds' timeout!' announced the head judge.

That was all the time Matt had to change Shawn's mind.

SHOWDOWN

'Can I speak to him?' Matt asked his captain.

'Sure,' said Lola.

Matt ran to Shawn. 'There's no need to throw it!' he said in a low voice.

'But he's putting bets on – if I don't stop him, he's going to clean up!'

'It's not worth throwing the fight for – c'mon, Shawn, I know you can win this bout *and* stop Fake-Wu.'

'But it's gonna take too long –'

'Just go for it, Shawn! Go for the win, and

then even if you lose you'll know you gave it your best shot.'

The buzzer sounded harshly. 'End of timeout!' called the judge.

Matt went back to his team. 'What'd you tell him?' asked Lola.

'I told him to go ahead and win,' said Matt simply.

Chang nodded in approval and Matt felt his chest swell with pride.

Back on the mat, Shawn's opponent came in fast to try to finish the bout he was so close to winning. His attack was too wild – Shawn deftly caught a flailing arm, turned into Mackenzie's body and sent him crashing to the mat with a lightning quick judo throw. He followed through and got Mackenzie in a neck-hold which, after five seconds, the judges called good.

Two points all!

Mackenzie came back, probing with some long-range kicks, trying to keep Shawn at a distance. Shawn avoided the first few strikes successfully. Mackenzie went for a flying kick, which would have flattened Shawn if it had connected. Shawn stepped nimbly back, caught Mackenzie's foot and flipped him on his back.

A huge cheer burst from the throats of the Beijing supporters.

But, Matt saw, they were behind in the cyber-battle. Fake-Wu looked happy – he must have got a heavy bet on. And with BIA 2–0 up, the odds looked good on him winning it.

Shawn practically sprinted back to his spot.

Catarina handed him the BlackBerry, shielding it with one hand. Shawn got busy at once.

'He's on another site to the one I wiped

133

before. I need to find him quick while it's still active – Matt, can you remember those websites we turned up in his study?'

'Sure,' said Matt, calling his photographic memory into play. 'Bets-Are-Us . . . Play-to-Win . . . Crazy Monkey Gambling Den . . . Double-or-Quits –'

'That'll do for starters,' said Shawn. 'Let's see now –' He clicked from site to site, then drew in a breath. 'Got it! Crazy Monkey! Look what he's doing – the bet I wiped before, he's put it on again here!'

Matt looked at the tiny screen in Shawn's hand. The characters glowed from a dialogue box: BET PLACED – 5,000,000 YUAN ON BIA TO WIN AT ODDS OF 4–6.

'Five million yuan!' gasped Matt.

'Not for much longer!' said Shawn with a grin. His fingers tapped on the keys and the figure in the box changed to 0,000,000 YUAN.

'Way to go!' said Olivier.

They all looked at the impostor. His mouth was open, his eyes wide with dismay. Matt saw that he was sweating; the make-up on his cheeks was trickling down inside his collar.

'He don't know what's going on!' giggled Catarina.

'What are you guys doing there?' said Carl loudly. 'Playing computer games? Can't you, like, support your team?'

'He's right,' said Lola. 'Come, we must show we are a team!'

'Right,' said Matt. If only he could explain! But it was impossible.

Singapore had just come back to win a bout, beating Andrei Drago. The Tangshan Tigers applauded him as he came back to his spot.

They clapped Abdul as he went out to fight the next bout.

Then Shawn returned his attention to the BlackBerry and the Tangshan Tigers craned to see over his shoulder as he pursued the impostor through cyberspace.

The two battles waged simultaneously. Matt did his best to concentrate on both, but his attention was drawn more to Shawn's BlackBerry, as the impostor went from site to site, trying to place a bet that would stay put. Shawn was almost keeping pace, but Fake-Wu was always a step ahead. Matt saw that his face was grim now, his lips compressed. He had clearly realized that someone or something was interfering with his gambling, although he had no idea who or what, and he was working faster and faster to find new gambling sites, get a heavy bet on and log out before it could be deleted.

Both Olivier and Catarina left with

reluctance to go and fight their bouts. They both won, and came running back.

The score in the tournament was 3–1, then 4–1, then 4–2, then 4–3, then 4–4.

Then Lola won her bout to take it to 5–4.

In the next bout Singapore got their own back by calling a timeout when Jahmal was two points up. The interruption put him out of his stride and Singapore went on to take the match.

5–5.

Carl was last up. His opponent was a tall Eurasian boy with a ponytail. He looked up for it, out on the mat quickly, bouncing on the balls of his feet as he waited for Carl.

'Good luck, Carl!' called Lola.

Carl glared at the Tangshan Tigers. 'You do realize it all hangs on this bout? And you're playing games!'

'Yeah, that's a bit bad,' said Andrei, and Abdul and Paolo muttered agreement.

'Sorry, Carl,' said Matt, looking up. 'Good luck, mate!'

As soon as Carl was out on the mat, however, the Tangshan Tigers huddled over Shawn's BlackBerry again.

Matt watched Shawn flip from site to site, looking for where Fake-Wu was trying to offload his stake now. It was his last chance and by the set, determined look on his face, he knew it. He wasn't even watching the tournament. Neither was Matt, though he was dimly aware from the shouting that the match was a close one.

'Got him!' said Shawn.

Matt saw that Fake-Wu had placed his entire stake, thirty million yuan, on the Win Win Win website. He was scrabbling furiously to log out before the bet could be wiped.

Shawn calmly hit a button and the figures winked out of existence.

Fake-Wu looked up as a huge roar burst out. Carl had knocked his opponent clean off the mat with a roundhouse kick to the chest.

The whole Beijing squad, Tangshan Tigers included, leapt to their feet and cheered.

Matt saw Fake-Wu look down at his laptop.

Fake-Wu's face froze. He let out a high, strangled scream. 'Noooooo!'

Everyone turned to stare at him in astonishment.

There was a dead silence.

Fake-Wu plucked nervously at his lower lip.

'Er – congratulations to my team for that very disappointing result – er, I mean very good result! Yes. Thank you.'

He jumped to his feet and strode briskly

to the door, laptop under his arm. At the exit, he looked over his shoulder and then broke into a run.

There was a moment's silence. Then a babble of noise arose again. Some of the crowd were chattering about the peculiar behaviour of their principal; others were still celebrating the victory.

Chang Sifu went across to speak to the Singapore coach. Perhaps he was explaining that he was sorry about bringing the tournament forward, that it wasn't his decision. Matt saw the opposing coach's face become friendlier.

Carl was still revelling in the congratulations of his team-mates.

'Come on,' Matt said quietly to the Tigers. 'Let's go and see where Fake-Wu's got to.'

They left the *kwoon* quickly and ran to the Principal's office.

The door was open a crack. Matt saw Fake-Wu sitting behind his desk, logging on to his PC. His hands were trembling.

He stared at the screen in front of him. He gave a loud, hollow groan and put his head in his hands.

Matt pushed the door open and the Tangshan Tigers followed him in.

'Is everything all right, sir?' said Matt brightly.

The side door to the Principal's office opened and Miss Lee, Wu's secretary came in.

'Is something wrong?' she asked. 'I heard a noise.'

'It was Mr Wu groaning,' said Catarina mischievously.

'You don't look yourself, Mr Wu,' said Miss Lee in a concerned tone.

'Hah!' said Olivier. 'You could say that.'

Miss Lee turned and looked haughtily at

the Tangshan Tigers. 'What are you children doing here, anyway?'

'We only came to see how Mr Wu is,' said Matt. 'Are you having trouble with your computer, sir?'

'I-I . . .'

From down the corridor they could still hear cheers coming from the *kwoon*.

'Shawn here could have a look,' said Olivier. 'He's a real expert on computers.'

'Glad to,' said Shawn, stepping forward.

'No, no, there is no need for that!' said Fake-Wu hurriedly, holding up his hands, palms outwards, as a barrier.

'Maybe if you took your glasses off you'd see the screen better?' said Matt. 'Because that's not really your prescription, is it?'

'What?' said Fake-Wu, startled. He put his hands up nervously to his face, leaving greasy fingerprints on the lenses of his spectacles.

'You might as well come clean,' said Catarina. She put her hands on her hips. 'We know you're not Mr Wu, it's totally obvious!'

'What do you mean?' said Miss Lee sharply.

'Look at his suit!' said Matt, pointing to the grey jacket draped over the back of Wu's chair. 'Would the real Mr Wu ever wear a cheap, off-the-peg suit like that?'

'There is nothing wrong with this suit!' said Fake-Wu defensively. 'It cost me —'.

'Mr Wu only wears tailored suits,' said Matt. 'Everyone knows that.'

'Yes, that is correct!' said a loud voice — and Mr Wu came rushing into the office in his dark blue overalls and workman's cap. Miss Lee gasped in shock. Their principal ran round the desk, caught the impostor by the throat and pushed him back against the wall.

'Kwan! I knew it had to be you!' Mr Wu cried.

'Get off me!' the impostor said, struggling.

'You came here – you tried to steal what was mine!'

His fingers tightened round Kwan's throat.

Matt and the Tigers jumped in. They grabbed Mr Wu by the shoulders, pulling him away.

'You are envious,' shouted Mr Wu, struggling against their hold. 'Envious of my success and you tried to destroy what I have achieved here!'

'So you want me to stay the poor relation all my life, do you?' said Kwan bitterly. 'Stay in the shadows and watch you lording it over everyone?'

'You should work, Kwan, if you do not want to remain a poor cousin!' shouted Wu.

So they were cousins, thought Matt. That accounted for the resemblance.

'Easy for you to say – you were born into

a wealthy family, your father pulled strings to get you this job.'

'I made the best of what I had and I am proud of it. Your parents had at least enough to give you a start in life, and you gambled it away in Las Vegas, didn't you?' Mr Wu spat the words out.

'I had bad luck . . .' his cousin protested feebly.

'Your bad luck is to be stupid!'

These words seemed to enrage Kwan more than anything else Wu had said. He flew at Wu and grabbed him. The pair of them wrestled in the middle of the floor, knocking over a chair. Miss Lee screamed.

Again, the Tangshan Tigers had to drag the two men apart. Matt and Shawn held Kwan by the arms; Olivier and Catarina clung on to Mr Wu's shoulders. The two men glared at each other.

'At least I have my own back on you!' panted Kwan. 'All the money I bet – it was your school's money and it has disappeared – thirty million yuan of your precious school's money! Who feels stupid now?'

'What?' Mr Wu went pale. 'Thirty mill– You-you –'

'It's all right,' said Matt calmly. 'The money was never bet. The school's funds are safe.'

'I deleted all the bets,' said Shawn. 'The money's all back in Kwan's account – easy to retrieve.'

An expression of agony crossed Kwan's face. The realization that he had thirty million yuan in his account that he would never get the chance to touch was clearly a painful one.

Mr Wu looked at the Tangshan Tigers as if he was seeing them for the first time. 'You – you have helped me greatly,' he said. 'Thank you.'

'*De nada!*' said Catarina.

'And you needn't worry,' said Shawn. 'We won't tell anyone about what happened. There won't be any scandal.'

'I will tell no one,' said Miss Lee.

'What about me?' said Kwan sullenly. 'If you're going to get all the money back, I'm off the hook, aren't I? You can let me go.'

'I do not think so,' said Mr Wu. 'It is a very unpleasant experience to be kidnapped.' He turned to Miss Lee. 'Would you phone the police? Ask them to send an unmarked police car. A discreet affair. I will explain when they arrive.'

An electronically amplified wind-chime sounded.

'Would the Principal and all members of the Beijing Academy martial arts squad please report to the *kwoon* for presentation of the trophy,' said Chang's voice over the tannoy.

'I must change!' said Mr Wu quickly. 'I cannot attend the ceremony in this disgusting boiler suit!'

'What about Kwan?' said Matt. 'Where can we put him? We don't want anyone to see the two of you together, or –'

'That is no problem,' said Mr Wu. 'I know a very good storeroom!'

As the Tangshan Tigers ran back to the hall, Matt called ahead to Olivier.

'Hey, Olivier – there's one good thing that's come out of all this.'

'What's that? You mean we saved the school's reputation?'

'No, I mean now all the fuss is over we'll be able to retake our exams in peace. Bet you can't wait to get back in the exam room!'

Olivier laughed. 'Yeah, the happiest hours of my life have been spent there.'

A cheer went up as the Tangshan Tigers entered the hall and joined the team at the side of the mat, next to Chang Sifu.

'Where have you guys been?' Carl demanded.

'Oh, just sorting something out,' said Catarina with a grin.

Mr Wu stood on a small podium by the judges' table. He was once again dressed in one of his sharp, tailor-made suits, a spotless white shirt and an impeccably knotted tie.

The head judge handed him the silver trophy.

There was another, bigger cheer as Mr Wu raised it for all to see.

'Congratulations to the gallant losers,' said Mr Wu, when the cheering had died down. 'I have been told – I mean, I know they fought with skill and commitment. And let me apologize for the bringing forward of the tournament, which was due to circumstances wholly beyond my control.

'Lastly, let me say a very big thank you to . . . to my team, who have surpassed all expectations. They have shown courage and loyalty, and, and . . .'

To Matt's surprise, Mr Wu's voice wavered and cracked. He took out a spotless handkerchief and wiped his eyes.

'Thank you,' he said quietly.

Catarina nudged Matt. 'Hey – you ever heard him like this before?'

'No,' said Matt. 'Never.'

'It's like he's learned what it's all about. I mean – well, you know what I mean.'

Matt did know. Wu had finally understood the true value of competing. It wasn't just about the glory of winning. It was about self-belief and not being cowed when the odds were against you – and sticking by your team.

'You have learned the biggest lesson of all,' said a quiet voice behind Matt.

It was Chang. Was he talking to Mr Wu? Or to the Tangshan Tigers?

There was no way of knowing.

There is one mystery the Tangshan Tigers will never solve, thought Matt. *And that mystery is Chang Sifu.*

He shared a private glance with the Tangshan Tigers. They smiled at each other. They'd helped win one more tournament. And they'd cracked one more case.

Matt looked round at the *kwoon*, full of celebrating BIA students. From across the hall, Johnny smiled and waved. *What a fantastic moment this is*, he thought. It meant the world to him, being part of this Academy; and being part of the martial arts squad; and best of all, being part of the Tangshan Tigers.

He saw Gianni Barenza crossing the hall to speak to him.

'Well done,' said Gianni, holding out his hand. Matt shook it. 'Tough fight, but you were better than me today.'

'Thanks,' grinned Matt. He glanced at Olivier, Shawn and Catarina once again. 'I couldn't have done it without my friends!'

Join the Team and Win a Prize!

Do YOU have what it takes to be a Tangshan Tiger?

Answer the questions below for the chance to win an exclusive Tangshan Tigers kit bag. Kit bag contains T-shirt, headband and cloth badge.*

1. What is the Chinese term for 'training hall'?
   a) *Kwoon*   **b)** *Karateka*   **c)** *Kufu*

2. Catarina's specialty is capoeira. Which country does this martial art come from?
   a) Britain   **b)** Bolivia   **c)** Brazil

3. In Karate, a sequence of movements performed without a partner is called *kata*.
   a) True   **b)** False

Send your answers in to us with your name, date of birth and address. Each month we will put every correct answer in a draw and pick out one lucky winner.

Tangshan Tigers Competition, Puffin Marketing, 80 Strand, London WC2R 0RL

Closing date is 31 August 2010.